W9-AKB-263

J
C

11,311

Carroll, Ruth (Robinson), 1899-
    The witch kitten.   N.Y., Walck, [1973]
unp.   illus.

1.Halloween-Stories.   I.Title.

EAU CLAIRE DISTRICT LIBRARY

For the children of St. Simons Elementary School,
St. Simons Island, Georgia

Library of Congress Cataloging in Publication Data Carroll, Ruth (Robinson) date- The witch kitten.
SUMMARY: A kitten that takes a wild ride on the witch's broom gets into all kinds of trouble.
[1. Stories without words] I. Title.   PZ7.C236Wi   [E]   73-7391   ISBN 0-8098-1206-1

Copyright © 1973 by Ruth Carroll. All rights reserved. ISBN: 0-8098-1206-1. Library of
Congress Catalog Card Number: 73-7391. Printed in the United States of America.

The Witch Kitten

RUTH CARROLL

EAU CLAIRE DISTRICT LIBRARY

Henry Z. Walck, Inc.   New York

76699